and Me

For Mum
– Sarah

Sarah Todd Taylor was brought up in Yorkshire and moved to Wales aged eight. She has had short stories published in several collections but *Arthur and Me* is her first book. Sarah loves to sing and when not writing she can be found singing opera around Mid Wales. She lives in Aberystwyth with her husband and keeps very cute hamsters. *Arthur and Me* won the Firefly Children's Book Prize 2014.

Peter Stevenson studied illustration at Manchester Art College, and went on to research folk drama and folk tale at Leeds University. He has illustrated, written and compiled children's books and fairy tales. As a storyteller he has told tales in church crypts, village halls, the hulls of trawlers, Greek tavernas, grand theatres, inglenooks, underground sewers, cafes, art galleries, working men's clubs, kitchen tables, leaking tents in hailstorms, and most recently in an inspiring allotment. Peter lives in Aberystwyth.

Arthur and Me

Sarah Todd Taylor

illustrated by
Peter Stevenson

Firefly

First published in 2014
by Firefly Press
25 Gabalfa Road, Llandaff North, Cardiff, CF14 2JJ
www.fireflypress.co.uk

A CIP catalogue record of this book is available from the British Library.

Print ISBN: 9781910080146
Epub ISBN: 9781910080153

This book has been published with the support of the
Welsh Books Council.

Typeset by Elaine Sharples
Cover design by becmadeappledesigns.co.uk
Dragonfly series design by Laura Fern Baker

Printed and bound by Bell and Bain, Glasgow

Chapter One

School trip accidents are not always my fault

One day I will go on a school trip without getting 'the talk' from Mrs Wendell-Jones. Not the one about turning up on time and bringing a packed lunch. The 'don't ruin this for everyone' talk.

'I don't want another accident, like the petting zoo, Tomos…' Mrs Wendell-Jones said, looking at me the way Mum does when she knows I've been up to no good.

'That rabbit could have bitten *anyone*,' I said.

'The soup factory?'

'I only leaned over the rail a little. They got me out of the soup very quickly.'

She breathed in really hard through her nose so that she made a 'phneeeeeee' sound.

'And WHAT about the safari park, Tomos?'

Ah.

Now the safari park was *possibly* my fault, but I didn't know what could happen. If I *had* known, I would most definitely *not* have fed my peanut butter chocolate spread sandwich to that giraffe.

'It cleaned off really easily, miss,' I said. Mrs Wendell-Jones wrinkled her nose at the memory.

Trust me. Giraffe sick smells utterly gross!

I knew Mrs Wendell-Jones was particularly keen

Sick Giraffe

I would behave on this trip, because we were going to the place where everyone thinks King Arthur is buried.

Mrs Wendell-Jones loves King Arthur. I mean *loves* him. She doesn't talk about anything else in class. She told us loads of stories about the Round Table and Camelot. She got us to cook old recipes that Arthur might have eaten (they were *not* nice). She even got us to learn some really weird old music that he might have sung. We don't get to do anything unless it's about Arthur.

Some of the stuff Mrs Wendell-Jones tells us is quite fun. I mean, the armour and the stories about all his fights with swords and big axes are ACE! She goes on and on about the Round Table though, as if furniture is super-dooper exciting. We have to build models of Camelot and draw the knights and their ladies, which is super-boring-dullsome-pants. So with Arthur being so dull, I thought nothing awful could possibly happen on this trip.

Nothing at all…

'Class,' Mrs Wendell-Jones said, beaming from ear to ear, 'you all know about our special trip next week. Now I have an even bigger surprise. This year our little school is in charge of the Harlech Schools' Eisteddfod and Mr Jenkins has agreed that we can have a special theme. Now, let me see if you can guess what that theme will b…'

'*King Arthur,*' everyone chanted.

Mrs Wendell-Jones clapped her hands. 'CLEVER children!' she cooed. 'There will be a poster about it in the hallway after class, so make sure you take a good look. Don't forget, there will be lots of bigger schools there, so let's make sure we make a special effort. We want a good turn out,' she paused, 'for Arthur.'

The Gruffudd twins laughed. Sharon leaned over to Bethan and made kissing noises. 'Ooh, Arthur, Kissy Kissy snooglecheeks,' she giggled.

Mrs Wendell-Jones heard her and looked very cross.

She thinks everyone loves Arthur as much as she does.

That would not be possible.

As we all went out for morning break I tried to imagine what awful competitions Mrs Wendell-Jones would dream up for an Arthur Eisteddfod. Pin the crown on the sleeping king perhaps, or best Arthur costume or…

'What's a juicing competition?'

Mair Gruffudd and her awful twin, Gwion, were crowding with the rest of the class round a poster that Mr Jenkins had put up on the wall.

'Jousting, you idiot, not juicing,' snapped Gwion. 'It's an Arthur thing. The knights would sit on their horses and clobber each other with long poles till one of them fell off.'

'You'd be good at that, Gwion. You like clobbering people,' said Mair. 'I bet you'll win.'

'I don't have a horse, though,' said Gwion.

'It says *bicycle* jousting,' Mair pointed out. 'You've got a bicycle. Nain bought you one for Christmas.'

Gwion looked really pleased. I knew he was already imagining himself winning. I didn't care. I bet it was a dull prize. Like a shelf full of books about Arthur or an Arthur dress-up costume or an Arthur action figure (if they made them) or...

'Tickets to see *PowerUp!*' shrieked Bethan.

'And meet the band!' yelled Mair.

What????

I pushed my way through the crowd. Everyone was getting excited about the poster now. I looked at Mr Jenkins' drawing of a knight in armour, looking really uncomfortable, and fighting what looked like a giant squirrel, but was probably meant to be a dragon (Mr Jenkins is NOT good at drawing). Above the squirrel-dragon's tail, in bright red, were the words, 'First prize – Meet Harlech's famous band *PowerUp!*'

Wow!

PowerUp are the coolest, most amazing band ever. I really needed to win that prize! Just for once I thought that Mrs Wendell-Jones was brilliant for liking King Arthur so much.

Then we went on the school trip.

There weren't any giraffes or vicious rabbits.

I could have coped with *those*.

Chapter Two

School trips are usually not as much fun as the teachers say they will be

'Caerleon is a wondrous, magical place, children,' Mrs Wendell-Jones gushed, waving her guidebook around in the air. She said there was an amphitheatre, and we thought she meant a huge one, like the gladiators used to fight in. There wasn't. There was a mound of earth that went round in a circle like a massive green doughnut, with a few steps and a bit of wall here and there.

Mrs Wendell-Jones stood in the centre of the doughnut, going on and on about Arthur and how he was meant to be fast asleep somewhere nearby. Everyone else just ran about, climbing on the doughnut or stabbing each other with pretend swords.

'Listen very carefully, class,' she called. 'You may hear the voice of Arthur on the wind.'

We all quietened down, even though we thought this was a bit dumb.

Then Gwion Gruffudd made a loud noise like a pig snoring and everyone laughed.

Everyone except Mrs Wendell-Jones. She looked a bit upset and told us we could have our lunch.

Mum had made my favourite sandwiches – peanut butter chocolate spread – and I sat down on the grass to eat them. I was about to take a huge bite when someone kicked me hard on the leg. Gwion Gruffudd stood over me with his mean face on. Gwion only has two faces – mean face and stupid face. If he has his mean face on, it means trouble.

'I forgot my lunch,' he said. 'So you'll have to give me yours.'

Gwion

Uh-oh.

'And it had better be a good one,' he said. 'Hand it over!'

I really wanted to say, 'No.' Mum's peanut butter chocolate spread sandwiches are so good (unless you're a giraffe). But I didn't want to spend the rest of the year looking out for spiders in my gym shoes so I handed my lunch over. Gwion looked at it, sniffed and stomped off.

I felt like everyone was watching. I wanted to go away and be on my own, where no one but me would be thinking what a sissy I was. I walked to the side of the earth doughnut and slipped out through one of the passages. Then I ran as fast as I could, putting awful Gwion Gruffudd far behind me.

Half an hour later I was lost.

In a wood.

Fairy tales get it wrong about woods. Woods are not magical, special places full of elves and helpful wood folk. They are just big clumps of trees. The most important thing to remember about trees is

this – they all look the same. When you put lots of them together it's very easy to get lost.

This is what I told myself. I was rehearsing what I'd tell Mrs Wendell-Jones, now she would be able to add 'got lost in wood' to my 'savaged by rabbit/fell into vat of soup/made a giraffe sick' list of reasons why I couldn't be trusted on a school trip.

'You see, Miss,' I said out loud, 'it's easy to get lost in a wood, because trees all look the

Saaaaaaaaaaaa....'

The last word came out as a long shriek, because the ground underneath me had stopped, well, being underneath me. I had fallen into a huge hole in the ground and was slipping down a long slope.

A really long slope.

Very very fast!

I tried to grab at the sides of the hole to stop myself from falling, but I just ended up with mud all over my hands as I fell deeper and deeper down.

Great.

Rabbit bites, soupy coat, giraffe sick and now stuck in a hole in the ground. This was definitely going on my end of term report.

Chapter Three

Lying to ancient kings might not be a good thing

'ZZZZzzzzzz … ngnnf … ngfff.'

I had landed on something, or rather someone, soft and furry.

Wherever I was, it smelled horrible, all cold and damp and dusty. It was also really dark. I squinted and could make out a few large mounds. They were snoring. Had I fallen into a bear cave? Did bears snore?

'ZzzzzZZZZ … nnngfft … my sword, mine! … give … zzzzzz.'

OK, bears might snore but they didn't talk in their sleep!

The mound that I was sitting on suddenly rolled itself over and I fell onto the floor.

'Zzz … zz … nfg.' The mound shook its head, the way my cat does when he's waking up. I looked around for an escape. The only way was to climb back up the hole and I wasn't sure that I could climb fast enough if the mound turned out to be non-friendly.

The mound opened its eyes and looked straight at me. It was an old man with a long beard and very bushy eyebrows. He stared at me.

'Is it time?' he asked. 'Do my people need me?'

Now where had I heard those words before? They seemed familiar. Were they in my favourite TV programme *Legend of Ulla*, or did Aramort Grout shout them as he conquered the universe in *Worldbuilders of Za'ark*?

Then I remembered. Mrs Wendell-Jones had told us about them. When she told us about Arthur being asleep, she said that when he woke up he would say to whoever woke him … oh!

'Are you Arthur?' I asked.

The old man nodded.

'Arthur Pendragon is my name,' he said, 'but some do call me Arthur, King of the Britons.'

I think that meant 'yes'.

'So these are…'

'My noble knights.' He sat up and looked around him. 'Why do they not wake?'

I shrugged. I had a brilliant idea. A really brilliant idea. Much better than any other idea I had ever had before.

'Did you ask if your people needed you?' I said.

'Yes,' he said. 'If I my people need me, then I am bound to protect them.'

Oh this was *awesome!!!!*

'I need you,' I said.

My super brilliant idea was – if Arthur taught me to joust, I'd be bound to win! Mrs Wendell-Jones had always been on about how Arthur was the best person at jousting ever. I could get him to teach me and then I'd beat the awful Gruffudd twins and win the joust and meet *PowerUp*.

Perfect!

I just had to get him home.

Arthur was still looking around at the other knights.

'They should wake too,' he said. 'When the great wizard, Merlin, sent us to sleep, he said that we would all wake when we were needed.'

'Urm…' I thought fast. My sister often sleeps

through her alarm, but Mum always makes me get up, which is mega-unfair. How come she gets to sleep on? Mum once told me she needed her beauty sleep. I said that no one could sleep *that* long and Mum got cross with me.

'Maybe they will get up later,' I said.

'Ah,' said Arthur, 'the magic rests more deeply on them.'

I nodded. He spoke in such an odd way. Not even Mrs Wendell-Jones was this posh.

Arthur heaved himself to his feet. It was like watching a mountain move – he was HUGE!

'So, young squire, what is your name?' he asked.

'Tomos.'

'And what do you ask of me?'

'I need to learn to joust!' I said.

'Ah,' said Arthur. 'Are you threatened by an evil foe?'

Hmm – foe? Ah yes, that meant enemy. I thought of the Gruffudd twins and nodded. *Boy*, was I

threatened by an evil foe! They were the most …
urm … foe-like people I'd ever met!

'Then lead on, young squire!' Arthur cried. 'We
will defeat them!'

Fantastic!!!!

I couldn't believe my luck. Arthur, actual Arthur,
King of the Britons, was going to help me to joust.
I was going to be the best jouster in the whole
school.

This plan could not fail.

Chapter Four

It's not always like they say it is in the history books

'Whatever you do, don't let anyone see you!' I warned Arthur.

We were standing by the school bus and I was keeping an eye out for the rest of the class. I didn't know how I was going to sneak him on board. Mrs Wendell-Jones was loopy, but even she would be able to tell the difference between a 10-year-old school kid and a bearded man wearing several layers of what looked like bearskin.

I'd just have to hope I was lucky.

I am hardly ever lucky.

'If you could tuck that beard in, it might help a bit,' I said.

Arthur looked at me. His eyes were as big as saucers. He pointed towards the bus.

'What is that?' His voice sounded like my mum's does when she's spotted something weird at the zoo. Of course! He'd never seen a bus before.

'It's a bus,' I said.

Arthur, King of the Britons

Arthur still looked confused. I tried again.

'Urm … it's like a … a…' I tried to think of something that Arthur would remember. 'A chariot! Yes, it's like a chariot.'

Arthur shook his head. 'But it has no horses.'

'It doesn't need horses,' I said. Arthur took a step backwards.

'Is it magical?' he gasped. 'You have magicians. Can they really make this move on its own without a horse? Merlin couldn't do it!'

That didn't sound right. Mrs Wendell-Jones told me Merlin could do *anything*.

'I heard he could teleport himself across the country instantly,' I said.

Arthur shook his head. 'Not at all, young squire, he was just a really fast runner.'

'He could change his shape into a bird or an animal.'

'He had a lot of pets,' said Arthur. 'He used to shoo them out in front of him when he left the castle. Sir Galahad laughed at him when he found out it wasn't magic. Let me tell you…'

'He fought a dragon!'

Arthur looked a bit embarrassed.

'What did you call this again?' he said, pointing to the bus.

'He *did* fight a dragon?' I insisted.

'A "bus"?' he asked, stroking one of the wheels.

'Well, did he?' I was getting really peeved now. He was definitely hiding something.

Arthur looked at his feet. 'It wasn't a dragon.'

Not a dragon?

'But Mrs Wendell-Jones told us…'

'It was a chicken,' he muttered.

No. Way!

'It didn't like him very much,' Arthur went on, 'and every time he came to Camelot it would attack him, so one day he…'

'Fought the mighty chicken.'

Arthur nodded.

25

'Poor chicken,' I said.

'Merlin lost,' said Arthur.

Lost?

'I'm not meant to tell anyone that. He told the knights how savage it was. They were all a bit nervous of it after that. Lucky for the chicken, really, it never got eaten.'

Merlin was turning out to be a bit rubbish, but all this was giving me an idea. I was going to ask Arthur lots about Camelot and Merlin and all the knights so I could get a good grade for The Big Arthur Essay.

The Big Arthur Essay was our end-of-term project for Mrs Wendell-Jones. She wanted us all to write what it would be like to spend a day in King Arthur's court. I wanted to write an awesome essay this time. All year I've got nothing but Cs and C+s and once even a C-. My soppy sister gets As all the time and once, just once, I wanted to be able to tell Mum I got a B and have her stick my essay on the fridge like she does with Soppy's.

I thought Arthur could tell me loads of amazing things about his knights. No one else would have someone who had actually *been* there telling them about King Arthur's court. I was going to get top marks for sure.

I was about to ask Arthur lots of questions, but

Mrs Wendell-Jones came round the corner with the rest of my class. She looked really worried.

'Look miss, there's Tomos!' Sharon yelled and Mrs Wendell-Jones stopped looking worried and looked very angry instead as she stamped over towards us.

'Where on earth have you been, Tomos? We were worried sick! I was just about to phone your parents and tell them that we'd lost you … again,' she said. Then she saw Arthur and stopped talking. I wasn't surprised. I bet a wrinkly old man in bearskins was the last thing she expected. Arthur bowed to her and took her hand to kiss it. Mrs Wendell-Jones leaned back slightly and looked a little scared.

'Arthur Pendragon, my lady,' he said, smiling broadly.

Mrs Wendell-Jones looked about to faint. Then she smiled back at Arthur and shook his hand so hard that I was surprised it didn't fall off.

'Of course!' she cried. 'You must be one of the tour guides. We were told that you might be in costume. What a shame we missed you, it would have been such a treat for the children.'

'I don't understand, my lady,' he said. 'I was found by this young squire...'

Mrs Wendell-Jones looked at me. 'Oh Tomos, *that's* where you've been. Learning more about dear Arthur, how good of you.'

Arthur looked very pleased at being called 'dear Arthur'. Behind Mrs Wendell-Jones I saw the Gruffudd twins scowling at me. They weren't happy that I was in her good books for once.

'It's *such* a shame we have to go,' she said to Arthur. 'It was so nice to meet you. Perhaps next time you could show us round.'

I thought super-dooper fast. I HAD to get Arthur on that bus.

'He's … coming home with me,' I said. 'He's … he's … a cousin!'

Mrs Wendell-Jones beamed from ear to ear. 'Wonderful!' she cried. 'We can talk all about King Arthur on the way home. What a treat.'

Everyone groaned. The Gruffudd twins looked daggers at me. Arthur looked quite pleased.

'I can tell you all some wonderful stories,' he said,

as Mrs Wendell-Jones guided him to the bus door.

I hurried behind them and tapped him on the arm.

'Arthur!' I whispered.

'Yes, Tomos?'

'Not the one about the chicken!'

Chapter Five

Turns out my room is full of magic!

On the way home, Mrs Wendell-Jones insisted that Arthur sit up front with her. He was talking to her all the way back so I thought she must be having a fantastic time, but when we all got off the bus at school she looked a bit puzzled. She stopped me as I was going down the steps.

'Tomos, does your cousin read a lot of books about Arthur?' she asked me. She was staring at Arthur in a very odd way.

'I think so, yes,' I said. 'He has to know all the stories so he can … um … talk to the visitors.'

'He told me the most extraordinary things,' she said.

Extraordinary – that's good, isn't it? It means better than ordinary, more than just the dull stuff everyone knows. I figured Arthur must know loads of cool stories about the old days. It was going to be so easy to get a good grade on that essay!

I raced home with Arthur. Well, I say 'raced'. It was pretty slow going actually. Arthur kept stopping and asking what everything was. I kept having to tell him that, 'Yes, everyone could afford a stone castle now, not just huts made of straw,' and explain what tarmac and cars and shops were.

When we got to my house I had to smuggle him inside. My sister was listening to her awful music, singing along with some of her drippy friends. My sister only listens to stupid boy bands who have spiky stand-up hairstyles and sing about how all girls are beautiful angels, which just proves that they have never met my sister. She isn't an angel. I think the goblins delivered her and then ran away to make sure that Mum and Dad couldn't give her back!

I told Arthur to follow me up the stairs quietly.

'Why?' he asked. 'Are we not welcome in this kingdom?'

'Not if my sister catches us, no.'

We tiptoed past her door and I threw open the door of my room.

'Sorry about the mess,' I said.

Arthur wasn't listening to me. He was staring, his mouth wide open.

'What is this place?' he asked.

'Urmm … it's my room.'

Arthur walked over to my computer and tapped at the screen.

'A dark mirror. Morgan the witch had one of these,' he said. 'She did her magic with it.'

Mrs Wendell-Jones had told us all about Morgan. She was Arthur's sister, sort of, and she was even worse than *my* sister.

'It's a computer,' I said, turning the screen on. A big picture of our cat, Mr Truffles, appeared on the screen.

'What magic is this!' Arthur shrieked and stumbled backwards, knocking over a pile of *Za'ark* action men that I'd left by my bed. Then he stood on them and started hopping round the room, clutching his bare toes and yelping.

I desperately shushed him, hoping that Soppy's music would be loud enough to drown him out.

Down the corridor, the music stopped.

I shoved Arthur, still clutching his foot, into my wardrobe and slammed the door. From inside I could hear his muffled voice.

'Ooohh … owwwwww!'

The door to my room flew open.

'What on *earth* are you doing, Tomos?' Soppy demanded.

Arthur howled.

'Arrrgh,' I wailed, trying to cover up the noise from inside the wardrobe. 'I, um, I stood on one of my action figures.'

She looked at me with disgust.

'You're wearing your shoes,' she sneered. 'You are such a baby! We are *trying* to rehearse.'

'Oooowwww!' howled Arthur.

'Oooararrghhhhhh!' I cried.

'So if you could keep the noise down, PLEASE!'

'Aaaargh!'

'Eaaaaaarghhh!'

She glared at me. She looked as though steam was about to come bursting out of her ears, or her head was going to turn round and round and explode (which would be SO COOL!).

'You are SUCH a child!' she yelled and stomped out, banging the door.

Arthur put his head out of the wardrobe. He had stopped wailing, but his eyes were so wide they almost met in the middle of his face.

'You have to keep quiet,' I hissed. 'If anyone finds you here we'll be in big trouble.'

Arthur nodded, clamped his mouth shut and made little whimpering noises. After a while he stopped grasping his foot and sat down on my bed.

'Are you a magician?' he asked.

I thought about this. I *did* have a magic tricks box that Auntie Jean bought me for Christmas, but I wasn't very good at it. No one ever picked the card they were supposed to, and I got my finger stuck in the machine that was meant to pretend to cut your finger off, and had to be taken to casualty.

They quite like me at casualty. All the nurses know me by now.

Then I realised that he was still looking at the computer. He thought that it was magic.

'This isn't magic, Arthur, it's just the stuff we have now. You've been asleep for ages,' I said.

'Stuff?'

'Things,' I said. 'Just things that we can make nowadays.'

'Tell me about them,' he said.

'I want you to tell me things,' I said. 'I want to know all about Camelot.'

Arthur looked surprised. 'Camelot? Why do you want to know about Camelot?'

So I told him about the essay and Mrs Wendell-Jones and about how I really wanted to get a good grade and prove to Mum and Dad that I wasn't bad at everything. I told him that Mrs Wendell-Jones had told us all about how brave and noble the knights were and how the Round Table had been created so that they would all be equal.

'No, it wasn't,' Arthur said.

'What?'

'It wasn't made so everyone would be equal. It

was made round because they all squabbled so much about who was most important that I got rid of my square one.' He sighed. 'I liked that square one, it had lovely carvings on it.'

The brave knights of the Round Table squabbling?

'Oh yes,' Arthur continued, 'they wouldn't stop bickering. Galahad was the worst. Always stirring things up, arguing with Sir Lancelot about who was the best looking and most popular. Sir Percival was always trying to get everyone to joust, and Sir Tristan just used to sulk and fire arrows at anyone who annoyed him. Awful, the lot of them.'

I was shocked. This was NOT the noble, gallant band of knights that Mrs Wendell-Jones had told us about.

'But they must have been brave,' I said.

Arthur nodded. 'Oh, they were all very good in a fight. Well, apart from Lancelot. He used to spend rather too much time looking at himself in his sword.'

This didn't sound right at all. Still, it must be true. I grabbed my pencil and a pad of paper and started scribbling it all down.

'Tell me about the day that you pulled the great sword from the stone,' I said.

Arthur looked puzzled. 'You mean the sword that made me king?'

'Yes, Mrs Wendell-Jones told us that only you could pull it out of the stone, and that proved that you…' I tailed off as Arthur's face went from 'slightly confused' to 'what on earth are you talking about?'

'You didn't pull it out of a stone?' I said.

Arthur pulled a face. 'Weeelllll, not really a stone. More a very large melon.'

'A WHAT???? Why did *that* make you king?'

Arthur shrugged. 'It was Merlin's fault. We were in the castle kitchen, and Galahad and Lancelot had been messing around with the great sword, and it got stuck. Merlin said, "Whoever can get that out deserves to be king," and just as he said it, I tripped over the melon and the sword shot out and hit Galahad on the knee.'

I stared at him. He looked a bit embarrassed.

'Merlin told me never to tell anyone that,' he said.

Too late. This was going in my essay.

'Tell me about jousting,' I said, flipping over a new sheet of paper.

The Sword
in the
Melon

Chapter Six

Even heroes get bullied

The next morning I woke Arthur up super early and snuck him out into the back garden. I had a huge surprise for him. I had made a jousting stand based on the pictures that Mrs Wendell-Jones had shown us in her books. I put a clothes airer at each end of our garden and balanced a broom between them. I was really pleased with it, but Arthur just grunted. He was bent over double holding his back because he hadn't slept well in my wardrobe and was a bit grumpy.

'It's my jousting lane,' I said. 'It's so you can teach me how to joust. We have to sit on our bikes and try to knock each other's hat off with these.' I waved a swimming pool noodle at him. They were the long foam rolls that Mum makes me use in the swimming pool till I learn to swim. Which I will do. Eventually!

Arthur was still grunting, so I ran over and got my sister's bike. I wheeled it over to him, hoping he wouldn't notice that it was pink and a bit on the sparkly side.

'What is this?' he said, straightening up a little.

'It's a bicycle,' I said. 'To ride instead of a horse. I'm sorry we don't have horses, but this is a special joust. I know you won't be able to ride a bicycle.'

'I can't ride a horse either,' said Arthur.

Eh?

'Fall off every time,' Arthur continued. 'And they make me sneeze.'

I decided that the only way to teach Arthur to cycle would be the way my dad taught me. So I took him up to the top of the hill by our house.

When we were at the top I told Arthur what to do.

'I'm going to let go, and I want you to keep pushing the pedals round so that you are cycling on your own. It's easy.'

Arthur looked a bit dubious, but he got on Soppy's bicycle and tucked his long robes round himself so they wouldn't get caught in the wheels.

'Ready?' I asked. 'Here we goooooo … STOP!!!!'

Arthur had pushed himself off down the hill. He

hadn't put his feet on the pedals, though. They were stuck out either side of him. He went faster and faster down the hill, crying out in horror and gripping the handlebars. I ran to try and catch up with him, but he was just going too quickly.

'Aaaaaargh!!!!' cried Arthur, wobbling all over the road.

'Hold on!' I yelled.

At the bottom of the hill Arthur hit the kerb and was catapulted into the air, over the handlebars, into Mrs Owen's rose bushes.

'Oooow!!!!' He screamed.

Soppy's bike was ruined. The front wheel looked like a floppy pancake, all bent out of shape. I was going to be in so much trouble for this.

Arthur sat in the middle of Mrs Owen's prize-winning roses. He had flattened a couple of the bushes and broken branches off the others. I really hoped that Mrs Owen wasn't home. If she caught Arthur sitting in her precious garden she would hit the roof. I leaned over and hauled Arthur out. He whimpered a little and grasped his bottom.

'The spines!' he yelped.

'We have to get out of here,' I hissed, grabbing his hand and trying to drag him. Arthur nodded and put one hand up to his head.

'Where's my crown?' he said, looking around him. 'It must be around here somewhere…'

He started patting the ground around him, lifting up decapitated roses and moving broken branches aside. I couldn't remember him having a crown on his head *before* he got on the bike. I wracked my brains trying to remember if I'd *ever* seen him wearing a crown. I closed my eyes tight shut and tried to see Arthur in my head. Yup, there he was. Brown furry robe, tight trousers, big boots with *far* too many buckles, long belt, rough shirt, long beard, grizzly face … and hair … and … YES! I was right.

'You didn't have a crown!' I said. 'I've never seen you wearing one.'

Arthur stopped patting the ground and looked up at me, astonished.

'What? I must have been wearing my crown.'

Half an hour later, after Arthur had uprooted nearly all of Mrs Owen's roses and Mrs Owen had chased us down the road screaming at us for what we had done to her garden, Arthur had to admit that maybe he *hadn't* been wearing his crown.

'It was a really nice one,' he sulked, stomping back towards my house. 'Everyone knew I was King when I wore my crown.'

I followed as quickly as I could. It's not easy to walk fast when you're trying to push a bike with a wobbly wheel. Soppy's bike kept wanting to go in a different direction to me and the chain had fallen off and was making a noisy clacking sound against the pavement.

'You're still King without your crown,' I said, trying to cheer him up. 'It must be brilliant being King, with everyone thinking you're great and listening to you and doing what you tell them to.'

Arthur shuffled his feet. He wouldn't look at me. He looked a bit like our cat does when it's done something on the carpet.

'Isn't it?' I asked.

Arthur mumbled something.

'What?'

'They don't listen to me.'

I was puzzled. 'Who doesn't?'

He looked straight at me and scowled. 'The knights!' he snapped. 'They never listen to me. They laugh at me. Galahad gets them to play games against me. Lancelot just does whatever he wants to and ignores me. Even Bedevere looks at me like I'm an idiot most of the time. You don't know what it's like.'

Wow! Arthur had his own set of Gruffudd twins to deal with. They sounded completely awful.

'Do they ever stick worms in your shoes?' I asked.

Arthur nodded. 'All the time. I had to fight an entire battle once with squelchy boots on.'

'What about ink down your neck?'

'Oh yes. Just as I was about to tell them off about the worms.'

'I get it from the Gruffudd twins,' I said. 'They steal my lunch too.'

Arthur looked down at me. He wasn't scowling anymore. He looked really sad.

'I need my crown, you see, Tomos,' he said. 'At least with my crown on I'm King. King Arthur. Without my crown, well I'm…' He looked down at the ground and shrugged. 'I'm nothing.'

I knew how he felt. Sometimes when the Gruffudd twins are bullying me, I feel like the whole world has turned round and is staring at me and thinking how stupid and small and useless I am.

'My mum tells me that it doesn't matter what they say. That words can't hurt me,' I said.

Arthur shook his head. 'That's not true. Words are powerful. Merlin made a spell once when we were being attacked. The castle was surrounded and we were in lots of trouble. Bedevere caught Galahad trying to escape through the garderobe.'

'What's a garderobe?' I asked.

Arthur went a bit pink. 'It's the … well, it's where you … it … urm…'

And then I remembered one of the trips to Harlech Castle with Mrs Wendell-Jones. The garderobe was a little cupboard for the loo. So Galahad was trying to crawl down the … EIWWWW!!!!

'Anyway, that's not the important part,' said Arthur, changing the subject so he wouldn't have to talk about poo-covered knights. 'We were going to be invaded so I asked Merlin for help and he got us all to speak words into a great cauldron. Nasty, mean words. Then Merlin cast a spell over them and told us to stand back.'

I leaned forward. This was the sort of story that Mrs Wendell-Jones would want to hear – ones with magic and battles. Definitely no weird killer chickens.

'When Merlin spoke, silver shards flew out of the cauldron, over the battlements of the castle and towards the invaders. They were sharp and fast and they drove everyone away. Merlin said that it was the words. Words had the power to hurt and push people away more than any metal on earth. He said that words are more dangerous than swords.'

I thought about all the times that I'd wanted to run away when the Gruffudd twins were shouting mean things at me. Merlin wasn't as daft as I'd thought.

Chapter Seven

Don't take ancient kings to school, it just causes trouble

The next day Arthur insisted on coming to school with me. He didn't want to sit in my wardrobe all day and he wanted to see some more of what he called, 'This amazing world you live in.'

Amazing?

School?

I had to dress him up in one of my school uniforms. He was amazed that I had one big enough for him. Mum has this really annoying habit of buying me school uniforms for at least four years ahead and making me wear them when they're HUGE so that I can 'grow into them'. Then, just as soon as they are the right size, she takes them off me because they are getting a bit worn! Parents are mad. Still, it did mean that I had a uniform that would fit Arthur. Well, almost.

'I look ridiculous in this,' moaned Arthur.

'You look fine,' I lied, jamming a baseball hat on his head and pulling the brim down so that his face was half hidden. Without all his robes and scratchy cloaks and leather coats, Arthur wasn't half as huge as I'd thought. He was a bit scrawny actually. He looked the way our cat did when we shaved all his fur off for an operation, with his legs and arms sticking out at odd angles.

I made sure we were at school early so that I could sneak him into my classroom. It felt a bit weird having someone sitting next to me and I really hoped that Mrs Wendell-Jones wouldn't notice that she had an extra person in the class. Arthur was trying hard to make himself small, but he almost had to fold himself in two to fit into the seat. His knees were pressed against his chin and his feet stuck out in front of his desk.

Everyone at school pretty much ignores me so no one noticed Arthur. The Gruffudd twins were too busy fighting over something to even look at me, but Gwion did remember to slap me on the back of the head as he passed my seat.

'Why do you let him do that?' asked Arthur, shocked.

I shrugged. 'Why do you let Galahad pick on you?'

Arthur frowned. He didn't get a chance to answer because Mrs Wendell-Jones breezed into the classroom, beaming from ear to ear.

'Children, I have some *wonderful* news!' she cried.

Oh great! Mrs Wendell-Jones' idea of wonderful news was always a bit different from our idea of wonderful news. I'll give you an example. My idea of wonderful news is that Mr Jenkins gives us a whole week off school, I get to eat peanut butter chocolate spread sandwiches every day and the Gruffudd twins have to move to Australia. Mrs Wendell-Jones' idea of wonderful news is that we get to walk round a boring old ruin, usually in the rain, while she tells us all about…

'Arthur!' Mrs Wendell-Jones announced.

'Yes?' Arthur said.

Mrs Wendell-Jones looked round in surprise.

'Who said that?' she asked.

Arthur stuck his hand in the air and waved at her. Mrs Wendell-Jones looked puzzled.

'I didn't think we had anyone new in our class', she said.

Arthur smiled. 'Ah,' he began, 'well I'm here because...'

'It's the school exchange!' I blurted out. 'With ... urm ... with that school in Caerleon.'

Mrs Wendell-Jones stared at me. 'I don't think I was told about this,' she said.

'I ... urm .... well Mr Jenkins organised it,' I lied, 'because of Caerleon being so important, you know ... urm ... Arthur.'

Mrs Wendell-Jones smiled.

'Well, it's always nice to have visitors,' she said. 'You must tell us all about Caerleon. How lucky to live in the place where dear Arthur sleeps.'

Arthur looked puzzled and said, 'Tomos' wardrobe?'

'Shhhh!' I hissed, but luckily Mrs Wendell-Jones had started to tell us all her big surprise. As well as the jousting tournament and the usual poetry competitions at the Eisteddfod there would be a special competition for the best Camelot costume.

'You can all dress up as knights if you like, although I'm sure some of you would like to dress up as Arthur himself,' she cooed.

They wouldn't if they knew what he smelled like, I thought! Hundreds of years underground does not make you smell great.

Mrs Wendell-Jones droned on for a bit, then she tried to teach us long division (which is really hard and I *bet* I never have to use it ever again). Then she collected up all our essays. I gave her a big smile as I handed mine over. I was sure I was finally going to get a good grade, with all the stuff that Arthur had given me. They were really good stories. I knew that Mrs Wendell-Jones would be impressed.

'What a lot you've written this time, Tomos,' she said. 'Our trip to Caerleon must have left a lasting impression.'

'Yeah, of Tomos' bottom in the hillside,' shouted Gwion.

I was trying to think of *something* to say back at him (and as usual I couldn't) and then the bell went and everyone got up for morning break. This was my chance to show Arthur the jousting lane, so I waited till everyone had left and then I dragged him off towards the gym.

We must have looked quite a sight, Arthur trying to bend himself in two so that he wouldn't look like an overgrown ten year old, me trying my best to look, what was that word Miss Hywel taught us — nonchalant. It means something like 'not caring and definitely NOT up to anything'.

Suddenly Arthur grabbed my arm so tight that I yelped.

'That *hurts!*' I complained.

Arthur didn't say anything. He was pointing at the Sports and Arts Trophy Cabinet and he was making these odd little burbling sounds.

'That's ... that's ... my... How *dare* they!'

I looked over at the trophy cabinet to see what he was so upset about. There were the sports day trophies for 'Best Sprinter', 'Best Team', 'Best Field Sport' and 'Best Trier'. I never won any of them, even Best Trier. I'm so bad at sports that even when I do try I somehow make it look like I'm not bothering. It's not my fault. It's just that my legs won't talk to each other.

It wasn't the sports trophies that were upsetting him, though. In the middle of all the 'Ooh, we're so good at sports and can run really fast unlike you losers' prizes (as I like to call them) was the Eisteddfod crown. It had the best place in the cabinet, on a stand, with a long list of all the people who had won it over the years for writing brilliant poetry. Soppy's name was on the list four times running.

Arthur pointed straight at it, his hand trembling.

'That's my crown!' he said.

Chapter Eight

Poetry can get you into trouble

'But *why* can't I just take it? It belongs to me!'

Arthur nagged me all break time about his stupid crown. At first he thought that I could open up the cabinet and just hand it over. I told him the cabinet had an alarm on it, which meant that I then had to explain what an alarm was. I didn't want him going on about magic again, so I said that there was a parrot that watched the cabinet and if anyone tried to get into it he would squawk really loudly. It's *sort* of how alarms work, I guess.

Then he came up with all sorts of ways that we could break into the cabinet. Most of them involved rocks.

'That's not going to work, Arthur.'

Arthur started to sulk. 'It's my crown. It belongs to me.'

And then I said it.

I really shouldn't have said it, but it just came out without me thinking.

'Well, you'll just have to win it back in the Eisteddfod.'

There it was.

Out there.

The most stupid thing I have ever said.

Arthur looked at me. 'The Eisteddfod? The gathering of the great bards? Is that what your teacher was talking about?'

I nodded. 'Yeah, there's a huge poetry competition. My sister keeps winning it.'

'And the prize is *my* crown?' Arthur asked. I nodded.

He stood up very tall and pulled his beard out of his shirt. 'Right,' he said. 'Thank you, Tomos. I must get to work at once,' and he started to walk off.

I ran after him. Where on earth was he going?

'If a poem will get my crown back, then I must write one,' he said, striding towards the school gates.

Hang on, he was meant to be helping me! This wasn't fair!

'But we've got to work on my jousting!' I said. 'We were going to look at the lane in the gym. You promised me you would help...'

He waved a hand in the air.

'My crown is calling me, young Tomos,' he said, not even looking at me (which is VERY RUDE) and he carried on walking. Of all the times to start acting like a King and throwing his weight around, he chose now! He had much longer legs than me, so I had to run to keep up with him. He got out of the gate and I was just about to reach him when...

'TOMOS! Where on EARTH do you think you are going?'

Mrs Wendell-Jones had seen me.

Chapter Nine

It turns out my sister is NOT the worst poet in the world

I was furious with Arthur all day. Mrs Wendell-Jones gave me a huge telling off and I thought she was going to keep me back after school and make me write something stupid like 'I must not leave school without permission' fifty times on a piece of paper till my hand ached.

I was wrong, though.

It was something worse.

The BIG ESSAY DISASTER.

Mrs Wendell-Jones handed out all our essays at the end of the day. She normally leaves little messages on them, like *'Excellent work, well done'* (I never get that), or '*More work needed*' (I've had that a few times), and sometimes '*See Me!*' which means that you're going to get told off BIG TIME.

My essay had '**SEE ME!**' written on it.

In capitals.

In red ink.

Underlined.

When the bell went at the end of the day, instead of going home, I went up to Mrs Wendell-Jones' desk.

She looked at me very sternly and waited till everyone had left before she started telling me off.

'What on earth were you thinking, Tomos?' she said. She looked very angry.

'Miss, it was a really good essay,' I said. Well, I DID think it was a great essay. I'd put all the stuff that Arthur had told me into it, and if anyone knew about life at Camelot it was Arthur.

But I couldn't tell Mrs Wendell-Jones that.

'A melon, Tomos?' she raged. 'The great Excalibur pulled out of a melon?'

'It was, Miss.'

'Bickering knights? Merlin fighting with barnyard animals? Knights crawling through the toilet?'

She was starting to do that odd 'breathing noisily through her nose' thing again.

I looked down at my paper. I had got an E minus. Hardly anyone gets an E minus. It's the worst grade it's possible to get. Mrs Wendell-Jones won't give out Fs because she says she doesn't believe in making us feel like failures. This just means that everyone knows that an E minus is really an F in disguise.

Not a very good disguise.

'Tomos,' Mrs Wendell-Jones said, looking really angry with me, 'the knights of the Round Table were noble, brave men. They didn't bicker or bully each other. Can't you see how ridiculous all the stories you have put in this essay must sound?'

This was stupid. My essay was the truth. It had to be. I couldn't argue, though, so I just nodded. Teachers are always right.

Even when they're not.

'Yes, miss,' I muttered.

Arthur was lying on my bed when I got home. There were bits of scrumpled-up paper all over the floor and he was frantically scribbling on a writing pad. When I walked into my room he glared at what he had written, tore it off the pad, scrunched it up and threw it across the room without looking.

It hit me in the eye.

'Ow!'

'Ah, Tomos. I'm glad you're back,' he said, sitting up. He waved the writing pad in the air. 'This is trickier than I thought.'

I glared at him. 'You walked off. I had no idea where you'd gone.'

Arthur looked hurt. 'I have to win my crown back, Tomos. Poems take ages to write, you know.'

So that was what he was doing – writing poetry. Well, I guessed it couldn't be any worse than Soppy's.

Wrong!

'Let me read you something I wrote earlier,' he said, searching through a pile of paper littered all over my bed. He seized one piece and waved it in the air. 'Here it is! Listen to this!'

I sat down and waited for him to start.

'I use my sword to fight my foes
I hit them on the head.
I slash them till their arms fall off
And pretty soon they're dead.'

He beamed at me. 'What do you think?'

Oh dear.

Something told me that Arthur's poetry was not going to win many prizes. This could get very awkward. I didn't like to think what Arthur might do if someone else won his crown – he might chop their arms off. It would be great if it was the Gruffudd twins, of course. I wouldn't mind him chopping their arms off. Then they wouldn't be able to pinch my lunch. But it wasn't likely to be the Gruffudd twins. It was more likely to be my awful sister. And she is awful but…

I didn't have time to think about his awful poetry now, though.

'You still haven't taught me to joust,' I said.

Arthur frowned. 'But my poems…'

'If you don't help me to learn to joust, I won't help you either,' I said, folding my arms and glaring at him. 'You can go back to your cave and you'll never have your crown ever again! So there!'

Arthur put down the paper and pulled himself off the bed. He looked a bit hurt and I felt bad.

'All right,' he muttered. 'But when I get my crown back you won't be allowed to shout at me ever again!'

He followed me into the back garden, grumbling loudly all the way.

Are all Kings this whiney?

Chapter Ten

There is only one thing worse than having one knight in your house

'You said you'd help!' I said.

I'd spent an hour cycling up and down the path trying to knock a hat off Arthur's head as he passed by. He was meant to be stopping me, but I could tell he wasn't trying. I had managed to knock his hat off every time, even though I was wobbling all over the place and had fallen over seven times.

The main thing I was learning about jousting was it's hard.

Really hard.

You have to ride your bicycle in a straight line holding the handlebars with one hand and a long wobbly swimming noodle in the other. You might as well ask me to juggle with jelly blindfolded on a unicycle. There was no way I was ever going to be good at this. It's sports. I'm rubbish at sports. If there was a medal for 'being a bit pants at sports' then I'd get gold every single year.

I could imagine myself standing in front of the Queen while she knighted me for 'services to falling over, coming last and generally being a bit rubbish.' Mum and Dad would wipe away proud tears and say to Soppy, 'If only you'd tried a little less, dear, you could be as terrible as your brother. Think how proud we'd be of you then.'

This never happens.

What actually happens if you are rubbish at sports is that the other kids laugh at you and Mr Deacon, the games teacher, just looks disappointed and says things like, 'I wish you'd try a little harder, Tomos.'

Is he joking? Has he no idea how utterly appalling I'd be if I stopped even *trying*?

What I mean is that I'm bad at games, and here was Arthur, who *was* a King, even if he was turning out to be a bit of a rubbish one, losing every single joust even though I was obviously Sir Terrible-can't-joust-for-toffee. I didn't think he was bothering.

'Does anything rhyme with chopped off?' he asked.

'Yes, plenty. Lopped off, for example,' I said. 'Why do you want to know tha... Are you *writing!!!*'

He looked a bit sheepish and tried to tuck a piece of paper into his shirt, but it was too late, I had seen it.

'You're meant to be helping me!' I said. 'All you can do is write your stupid poems. It's not fair!'

Arthur wasn't listening to me. He was staring over my shoulder at something at the end of the garden.

'I don't believe it,' he muttered.

I ignored him. 'You'll never win, you know,' I snapped. 'Your poetry is even worse than my soppy sister's! Who on earth wants to hear about how you chop people's heads off? I bet you didn't. I bet you just hid while everyone else did the brave stuff!'

Arthur looked really hurt but I was so angry I didn't care. I just kept on yelling at him.

'Do you think that people really want to hear poems about your stupid knights being horrid to everyone, or about how you couldn't get them to do anything, or about how no one liked you?' I yelled. 'Let's see what your latest one is about, shall we?'

I snatched at the paper he had tried to tuck inside his shirt. Arthur grabbed at it, but he wasn't fast enough and I opened the paper and read it aloud.

'I wish I felt more like a King
I wish that I was brave
I like to run about and sing
That's not how Kings behave.'

'HAH!!!!'

Behind me, someone laughed out loud. Then more people laughed and shouted things like 'Rubbish' and 'Typical Arthur!' and 'What a wuss!!'

I turned round.

At the end of the garden there was a group of men dressed in armour. The tallest one had long blond hair down to his shoulders. He was very handsome, but he looked really mean.

'Oh no,' Arthur said. 'It's Lancelot!'

'So this is where you are, Arthur,' the tall knight said, striding down the garden like he owned the place. 'Time to go back. You shouldn't have left without us.'

'Well, when young Tomos said that he needed me I answered his call,' Arthur said. 'Naturally I thought my knights would follow…'

'Follow you?' laughed Lancelot. 'Why on earth would we follow you?'

Arthur looked really upset. 'I *am* your king,' he muttered.

'Where's your crown?' one of the other knights demanded. He was a short squat one with really dirty hands and a grumpy look on his face.

'Can't be king without a crown,' another said. 'It's … what's the word … a bit like sick budgie.'

Lancelot rolled his eyes. 'Illegal,' he muttered.

The other knight nodded. 'That's the blighter!' he said.

'It isn't illegal,' I objected. 'We've got a Queen and she doesn't wear her crown all the time. It's kept safe for her in the Tower of London. She's still Queen.'

Lancelot glared at me. 'I don't think I was talking to you.'

Illegal

I shut up. He looked like the 'hang you by your trousers from a tree branch' type.

'Anyway, Arthur,' Lancelot said, running a hand through his hair and looking really bored with this conversation. 'Now we've found you...'

'Yes, how did you do that?' Arthur asked. 'Merlin is gone. His magic is no longer here, how did you...'

Lancelot sighed and drew a piece of paper out of his pocket.

'Your little friend left this in the cave. Once we knew where to look, we just had to follow the sound of utter stupidity and there you were!'

It was a menu for our local pizza place, the one that does the triple pepperoni with pineapple that I love. It must have fallen out of my pocket when I landed in the cave.

Lancelot flung it lazily at me.

'You have to come back with us now,' he said to Arthur.

For a second I thought that Arthur was going to say no and stand up for himself. He pulled himself upright and looked Lancelot straight in the face. But then his lip trembled and his shoulders slumped

down again. He made the tiniest of head movements, one that might, when it grew up, be a nod.

I couldn't believe he was letting this overgrown bully boss him around. He was a *king*! I stepped forwards, reached up and poked Lancelot in the chest.

'I've got something to say to you,' I said, trying to sound braver than I felt.

He looked down at me and laughed. 'Oh yes?' he said, looking around at the other knights with an 'Ooh, I should be sooooo scared' look on his stupid face.

'Yeah,' I said. 'What I want to say is … is … is … blimey, my dad's home!'

That wasn't what I'd meant to say. It was true though. My dad was walking towards the house. There was no way I could explain why I had a dozen knights standing around the garden. I had to hide everyone quickly. But where? I couldn't get them into the house. Soppy was in there. I couldn't get them out of the garden without Dad seeing them. That left only…

'Get in here, quick,' I yelled, pulling open the door of our garden shed.

The knights stared at me.

'It's … urm … it's a magic portal to get you back to the cave!' I cried. 'Yes, that's what it is. Just walk inside and you'll find yourself in the cave in no time.'

Lancelot didn't look convinced.

'Is this true?' he said to Arthur.

'Well…' Arthur began.

Oh pleeeeeeeease hurry up, I thought, *Dad will be here any second now.*

'He certainly has great magical powers,' Arthur said. 'Better than Merlin.'

That was enough for Lancelot. He waved at the knights to go into the shed and they piled in. I waited till they were all inside and then slammed the door and padlocked it shut. From the inside I could hear muffled cries.

'Hey, why aren't we at the cave?'

'You're standing on my ear, Galahad!'

'Where has that wretched child sent us?'

Hoping that Dad wouldn't be able to hear them, I went to take the brooms off Mum's clothes' horses. I would have to find a way to get rid of the knights, but keep Arthur. Surely I could figure that out.

From the shed I heard more cries.

'Isn't it dinner time? I'm hungry.'

Uh-oh.

Chapter Eleven

Knights cannot be kept as pets

'There was an entire chicken in here this morning!'

Mum was staring inside the fridge. I knew what she was angry about. The chicken had been for lunch with Nain. The problem was I had all these hungry knights to feed. I had to keep them quiet while I figured out what to do about them, and they ate a LOT. When I took them the chicken all they did was complain.

'Just one?' Galahad had said. 'We meant one each!'

Mum knew that I'd taken it. She glared at me, waiting for an explanation.

'Urm, it was…'

And then I did the most disloyal, traitorous, treacherous thing I have ever done in my entire life.

I blamed it on Mr Truffles.

'I was just moving it around in the fridge, you know, to fit the milk back in, and Mr Truffles jumped up, grabbed the chicken and ran off with it. Sorry, Mum.' I tried to look suitably sorry in an 'it wasn't my fault, you know what cats are like' sort of way.

Mum calmed down a bit.

I'd have to find a way to make it up to Mr Truffles later.

I went out to the garden to see how the knights were getting on in the shed. It had been two whole days and

so far all they'd done was bicker. Except for Bedevere. He turned out to be very good at crafts and had used my Dad's tools to fix the shelving and make a few more chairs for them to sit on from old paint cans.

'…and I think that we should just break the door down and find our own way back,' came a voice from the shed. It sounded like Sir Lancelot. He was always bossing the others around. He and Soppy would make a brilliant pair.

'But Arthur says the boy is a great magician. He could be powerful.' That was Gawain. I quite liked him. He was the best of the bunch anyway.

'Like Merlin?'

'No, I said a great magician.' Yup, that was definitely Gawain. He made me laugh.

All the knights started talking at once.

'You leave Merlin alone. You were always mean to him.'

'To be fair, he was a bit rubbish. If it wasn't for him and that melon…'

Sir Gawain

'Well, if you hadn't annoyed that chicken…'

I knocked on the door and they all went quiet. Then Lancelot said, 'Tomos, let us out at once or you will be very sorry.'

'I want to talk to King Arthur,' I said.

'If you open this door, we'll push our way out,' said Bedevere.

I heard a loud noise like someone being hit over the head and then an 'Ow'.

'You're not supposed to tell him the plan, you idiot!' hissed Lancelot.

This was a problem. If I opened the door they'd all get out, but if I didn't then I wouldn't be able to talk to Arthur. I really needed him. The joust was tomorrow and I still had no idea what I was doing. I'd tried to practise on my own, but I didn't have anyone to aim at so I wobbled all over the place and fell off. Arthur must remember *something* about the way the knights used to do it, even if he was a bit useless himself.

How on earth was I going to get the door open without all of them rushing out? I remembered that they all believed that I was a great magician. Hmmm, could I use that somehow?

'Sir Lancelot,' I said in what I hoped was a brave imposing way, lowering my voice so that I would sound a bit older.

There was a pause.

'Does the child have a cold?' someone asked.

I chose to ignore that.

'Sir Lancelot,' I went on, 'you will not have been able to use the ... um ... the portal to return to your cave yet because I lack one element needed for the spell to work. King Arthur must come out here and assist me.'

I crossed my fingers behind my back, hoping they'd believe me. People don't often believe me. I'm really bad at lying. My face goes bright red and my nose twitches.

There was a frantic muttering inside the shed. I tried as hard as I could to hear what they were saying, but I couldn't. Eventually Lancelot rapped on the door.

'Are you still there, child?'

'Yes,' I said.

'Answer me this, then. Why shouldn't we just overpower you and go back to the cave the way we came?'

Ah! I'd been hoping they wouldn't ask *that*. I thought quickly. Mrs Wendell-Jones must have told us something I could use. Something that the knights feared more than anything. A monster? That massive Green Knight that Sir Gawain had been terrified of? Or Palaug's Cat, the scary beast that Sir Cei had killed? Maybe I could convince them that Mr Truffles was Palaug's Cat come back to life and then they would stay in the shed in fear for their lives.

I looked over at Mr Truffles sprawled out on the grass, snoring gently in the sun. Yeah, that wasn't going to work.

Then I knew.

I took a deep breath to make my voice sound *especially* scary and said, 'I saw Merlin's chicken in town yesterday.'

There was a gasp and then more muttering. Part of me couldn't believe this was going to work. Surely they couldn't really be scared of a little chicken? I heard Lancelot cough and tap on the door again.

'Child?' I hated how he called me that. It's like when Soppy calls me 'squirt'. Really annoying.

'You can have Arthur,' Lancelot continued, 'if you promise to have us out of this hut by sundown.'

'No problem,' I said. 'I promise. Now send forth the noble Arthur, please.'

I'm sure I heard them sniggering at that. There was a bit of a scuffle as the knights all rearranged themselves to let Arthur squeeze through and then I heard Arthur's voice.

'You can let me out now, Tomos.'

As I opened the door of the shed, Arthur tumbled out and fell onto the floor in a heap. Inside the shed the knights were perched on shelves, Dad's workbench and the paint-can chairs that Bedevere had made.

'Sundown, remember, child,' Launcelot warned me. 'You have till sundown.'

I nodded. That was all the time I needed.

Chapter Twelve

Blindfold jelly juggling is probably easier than jousting

'Right,' I said to Arthur, 'you know what we have to do *now*.'

'Run away?' Arthur suggested.

'No,' I said. 'You are going to help me to joust and you are going to help me now.'

There was more sniggering inside the shed. I saw Arthur's shoulders slump.

'And we are going to ignore those idiots in there,' I finished, walking off to the end of the garden to set up the jousting lane.

Galahad stuck his head out of the shed window and shouted at me, 'Hey, boy! I hope you've put padding on him. The only thing he knows is how to fall off.'

He pulled his head back inside and there was loud laughing.

I kept on walking. I didn't need to look back at Arthur to know how he must be feeling. I set up the jousting lane and got my bike. Soppy's bike was in the shed with the knights, hidden at the back. When she found out what had happened to it, I was going to be in big trouble.

Once I'd got everything ready, I dragged Arthur over and we started to practise.

I was still useless. I kept falling off into the rose bushes or dropping my noodle-lance, or wobbling in a wonky line and running over Mr Truffles' tail.

After an hour I was covered in rose thorn scratches, mud and cat bites.

'This is hopeless,' I grumbled.

Arthur sat down on the ground. 'I don't think I've been much help to you, young Tomos,' he said, picking at the grass and not looking me in the face. 'Perhaps I should have gone back to the cave when you suggested it.'

'You must remember *something*,' I said. 'I mean, Mrs Wendell-Jones says that you were this great jouster.'

'You have got to be *kidding!*' came a cry from the shed. The knights started sniggering and then

laughing louder till it sounded like I had a hundred hyenas trapped in there.

'Arthur, a jouster?' said another knight. 'He couldn't joust his way out of a hessian sack. He used to flee when he saw a mouse in the kitchen. That's what he was running from when he tripped over the melon.'

I looked at Arthur. He looked more miserable than ever.

'Is that true?' I asked.

He nodded. 'Yes, Tomos, I became King of the Britons because I ran away from a mouse and tripped over a melon.'

I stared at him. As the laughter in the shed grew louder and louder, Arthur seemed to shrink towards the ground, his whole body sagging and trembling a little.

'Arthur, are you…' I stopped myself just in time. No one likes to be asked if they're crying. Not when they are.

'Brave King Arthur,' came a mocking voice from the shed, 'afraid of a little mousekins.'

Arthur sniffed.

Right.

That.

Was.

IT.

!

I stood up and gave my shoulders a huge 'I mean business' shake, like they do in films when they're about to be super-brave, and marched over to the shed. Galahad and Lancelot were each peering out of a window, laughing their heads off.

'Uh-oh,' Galahad giggled. 'We're in trouble now. Look who's coming to fight Arthur's battles for him.'

I stood underneath the window and glared at him.

'Scared of a mouse is he?' I yelled. 'Well, how about I go get Merlin's chicken and we'll see just how brave some of you are?!'

Galahad stopped laughing.

'Yeah,' I jeered. 'You all think you're so tough, but look at you. Twelve noble knights giggling like idiots in a shed! How long is it since any of you did anything brave, huh? Arthur came out here *even though* the dreadful Chicken of Doom could be just round the corner. He's braver than the lot of you put together. He's been to school with me. He faced Mrs Wendell-Jones. He's trying to help me. We might not get very far, but it's better to try than just to stand by and laugh and be mean and spiteful. Mrs Wendell-Jones told me that Arthur's knights were brave, fearless, noble, kind and loyal, but you're not.

You're a bunch of lily-livered cowardly selfish mean idiots. None of you deserve to be called a knight!'

After I'd said all that, I noticed no one was laughing anymore. Galahad and Lancelot pulled their heads inside the shed and shut the windows tight.

I took a deep breath. My hands were shaking. I didn't feel very brave anymore. What if they all burst out of the shed together and attacked me?

I waited. The shed was silent.

I heard a sound behind me and turned to look at Arthur.

He was staring at me with his jaw wide open and his eyes big and round. He looked like my mum and dad look when Soppy gets her exam results.

'That was amazing,' he said. 'Tomos, you're so...'

'Stupid?' I offered.

Arthur shook his head.

'I was going to say brave.'

Chapter Thirteen

It's easier with the right stuff

When I woke up the next morning I remembered that the joust was today and I was nowhere near ready. The entire school was going to be there to see me fall off my bike and make a fool of myself. Worse still, I was going to have to watch Arthur read some of his terrible poetry. In public. This was officially the worst day of my entire life. I pulled the bedclothes over my head and tried to think how I could get out of it.

'Wake up, sleepyhead, it's a big day,' shouted Mum from downstairs. 'And don't take too long in the bathroom!'

Fat chance. Every morning Soppy takes over the bathroom and spends *forever* in there. By the time she's done, I usually have about five milliseconds before we dash off to school. Then Mum complains that I haven't brushed my teeth properly. If all my teeth fall out before I am fifteen, I will blame it on my sister and her stupid floral bath bombs.

I rolled out of bed and went over to the wardrobe to wake Arthur. The door was wide open.

Arthur was gone.

He'd left me. On the day of the joust. Maybe he'd run back to the cave to get away from the awful knights.

He hadn't said goodbye.

I couldn't believe it. My last chance to learn how to joust had just gone. The whole school was going to watch me fall off my bike and get clobbered by Gwion Gruffudd and I was going to get laughed at again.

Because that's what I do best. I fail and I get laughed at. So I might as well get it over and done with.

I got dressed and went over to draw the curtains and that's when I saw it.

In the garden.

A perfect joust lane.

It wasn't one of Mum's brooms wobbling on top of the clothes airers with its bristles sticking out at odd angles. It was a long, straight wooden beam that ran down the middle of the path. At each end there was a long pole with a flag fluttering in the breeze.

It looked just like the pictures in Mrs Wendell-Jones' books.

I dashed down to the garden and ran up and down a few times, pretending I was on my bicycle, or even a horse. It looked even better close up. It had things carved into the wood, pictures of knights riding in armour, holding out their lances towards their opponents. Each of them had a flag waving above his head. I peered closely. They had names carved onto the flags.

Sir Bedevere.

Sir Lancelot.

Sir Gawain.

Oh!

At the end there was a shorter knight. Instead of a horse he was riding a bicycle. His flag read *Tomos the Brave.*

Oh wow!

'Bedevere made it,' said a voice. I turned round and there was Arthur, with all the knights behind him. They weren't looking as mean as they normally did. Some of them were even smiling.

'He stayed up all night finishing it so we could teach you how to joust properly,' Lancelot said.

I stared. 'You'll teach me?' I said. 'Really?'

'You don't want that lane to go to waste, do you, lad?' Sir Gawain laughed.

I looked at the jousting beam. It looked really good. I wondered where they had got the wood from.

Then I noticed that our garden table was missing.

'Come on, Tomos,' Arthur said. 'Let's try it out. Show them what you can do.'

He grinned at me. I wanted to do really well, to show the knights that Arthur had taught me *something* and that he wasn't completely useless. I grabbed my bike and set it up at one end of the long wooden beam.

Sir Lancelot walked over to the other end and stood ready. He was pushing…

'That's Soppy's bike!' I said.

It *was* Soppy's bike, only it wasn't all buckled and bent out of shape anymore. The frame was straight and the wheels were perfectly round. It didn't even make a squeaking noise when Lancelot wheeled it.

'He can fix anything, can Bedevere,' Arthur said. 'Merlin says he has magic hands.'

Lancelot dropped his metal visor over his eyes and climbed up onto Soppy's bike. He wobbled a bit, but I suppose he'd never ridden one before.

Arthur helped me onto my bike and handed me the swim-noodle.

'Right,' said Gawain, 'what you need to do now is *not* look at Lancelot.'

'What?' I said. 'But how am I going to hit him if I don't look at him?'

'Ah,' said Gawain, 'if you look at your opponent you won't concentrate on staying solidly on your horse. Stare straight ahead of you and keep your lance … well … your … whatever that is, keep it out to the side so that it knocks him off, but *don't look at him!*'

I nodded. Don't look at Lancelot. If that was all it took then it shouldn't be too tricky. I clambered onto my bike and waited for Arthur to give the signal.

Jousting is AWESOME!!!! Really really awesome.

You can go mega-fast once you practise, and Gawain's tip really worked! We practised for ages and I was getting pretty good at it. I'd *almost* knocked Lancelot on the head loads of times. I figured if I could be this good against Lancelot, a great knight who had fought in *real* jousts with *real* horses and real lances, then it was going to be no problem winning against a load of school kids on wobbly bicycles.

'You nearly had him that time,' Arthur told me, beaming proudly as I cycled back to the start of the lane to have another go.

I nodded. 'I'm doing everything that Gawain told me to,' I said. 'I don't know though, I just can't quite manage to…'

I tailed off. Who was I kidding? I was never going to beat Lancelot. He was probably pretending to almost lose just to make me feel better. I bet behind

my back all the knights were still sniggering about how dreadful I was.

All of a sudden it didn't seem so awesome after all.

'I'm never going to win, am I?' I said.

'What sort of talk is that?' Arthur said. 'Is that the young knight who stood up to the entire Round Table?'

I shrugged. Arthur took me by the shoulders.

'Now you listen to me, Tomos. That lot have never worked together on *anything*. They bicker and they fight and they lost loads of battles because they wouldn't work together. Now look at them. They're helping you and they haven't tripped each other up or thrown things around once this morning. You did that. You. I reckon if you can do that, then you can do pretty much anything!'

I looked over at the knights. They didn't look like they were laughing at me. Lancelot was waving at me while Bedevere helped him balance on Soppy's bike. Gawain was keeping watch for Mum and Dad. The others were lined up along the joust lane smiling at me.

They looked like they were on my side.

'OK,' I said, 'I'll give it another go.'

I took a deep breath and leaned forward on my bike so that I could get up a good speed. I careered down the garden towards Lancelot and, just as I got within a few inches of him, I swung my swim-noodle at him and…

…I knocked Sir Lancelot off his bicycle.

I actually knocked him over.

WOW!

'This is going to be ace,' I cried, jumping off my bike. 'I reckon I'm going to win. You all have to come and watch. Promise you will.'

Lancelot sat up, rubbing his head. 'Tomos,' he said, 'you are going to be … what is that word you use … brilliant.'

I grinned. 'I am, aren't I.'

This was going to be great.

Chapter Fourteen

What is a hero?

The castle was stuffed full of people by the time we got there. Mum and Dad came with me and I told Arthur and the knights to sneak out of the garden and follow on afterwards. Half the town was dressed as a knight or a medieval lady so I figured they wouldn't be out of place.

Our castle is the best one in Wales. You can climb right up to the top of the walls and look out for miles. There's even a big ditch like a moat round the outside and a sort of drawbridge. It's loads better than any of the other castles.

Everyone in town had turned up early for the Eisteddfod. Mr Jenkins had let Mrs Wendell-Jones go to town on decorations. Round the inside of the castle walls there were stands like medieval stalls selling bows and arrows, wooden swords and stuff like that. There was even a man from the local wildlife centre with a falcon on his arm. A real life falcon! Awesome!

Mrs Wendell-Jones was standing on a wooden platform in the middle of the grounds, pulling some red cloth over one of the school chairs made up to look like a throne. She was wearing a dress like Maid Marian wore in my Robin Hood book and she had this huge hat on, a long cone with some glittery cloth hanging from it. It made me want an ice cream.

'Tomos! How lovely to see you,' cried Mrs Wendell-Jones stepping carefully down from her platform. 'And what a wonderful costume. You look just like a noble knight.'

I grinned. Mum had made me a great costume. It was made of cereal packets covered in tin foil and strung together so it was hinged like real armour. She had bought me a helmet too, with a visor that went up and down, and had got an old pair of boots and spray-painted them silver. I thought I looked great.

'So, is the noble knight ready for the joust?' Mrs Wendell-Jones waved her hand over to a spot by the wall of the castle where the old hall used to be. There was a jousting lane all set up ready for the competition.

I nodded.

I was ready.

Mr Deacon had drawn everyone's name out of a hat that morning to decide who would face who in the first round of the competition. I was drawn against someone called Owain from the secondary school. He was easy to beat. He got on his bicycle, picked up his noodle-lance, lost control and rode straight into the crowd watching us. I managed to beat a few other kids.

Then I had to face Sharon Jones. She was really good. We rode up and down the lane four times missing each other by inches before I finally managed to knock off the sponge ball that was velcroed on top of her helmet.

'Wow, Sharon, you nearly got me then,' I said as we walked away from the jousting lane.

Sharon shrugged. 'Well, I suppose I'm lucky really,' she said. 'I wouldn't want to face Gwion Gruffudd in the best of three.'

What?

I looked over at the leader board next to the jousting lane. Gwion was about to challenge Dafydd Baker and I was going to have to face whoever won. I'd been watching Gwion joust and he was very good, even against the bigger kids. He was fast on his bike and he had strong arms from all those years of holding little kids up against the wall to get them to give up their pocket money. Whenever he managed to hit someone with his swim-noodle, he didn't just knock the ball off their head, he usually knocked them off their bike too.

Yikes.

I really needed some advice from Galahad or Lancelot. What was that move that Lancelot had shown me? The one that had helped him defeat the great Knight of Monmouth. If I could try that one on Gwion, then maybe I could win.

I was just going to look for the knights when Mum grabbed my arm and dragged me over to the poetry podium. Soppy stood there, clutching a huge pile of paper. There was a big crowd gathering. Everyone loves the poetry competition. Mum is always going on about how brilliant it is that Soppy writes poetry. She calls her 'our little bard' and shows every visitor the prizes that Soppy has won with her amazing poems like 'Hammy Hamster's Day Out' and 'Bestest Friends Forevermore'.

Soppy went first. Her poem was about wanting to be a star when she grew up and it went on for ages! Even Mrs Wendell-Jones stopped smiling after the first ten minutes. A few people wandered off in the middle and I saw Dad yawn before he was jabbed in the ribs by Mum. When she *finally* finished everyone clapped politely and Soppy swanned off to sit down on one of the chairs at the side of the stage.

Mrs Wendell-Jones looked down at her list of competitors. 'Seren Jones, please,' she called out.

Seren stood up and read out a poem about her pony and then there were a few poems about 'summer holidays' and 'my cat' and then Mrs Wendell-Jones called Arthur's name.

Arthur walked slowly to the middle of the stage and coughed a few times. I waved at him and he smiled and coughed again.

'Urm…' he began.

Mrs Wendell-Jones patted him on the shoulder.

'No need to be so shy,' she said, 'just think of all your friends wanting to hear your splendid poem. What a wonderful costume too, very convincing.' She tugged on Arthur's beard, which made him wince. 'Your mum should be very proud of you,' she said, and she pushed Arthur to the front of the stage.

'Urm…' he said again. 'My poem … my poem is called Heroes,' and he began.

'What is a hero?
Strong and brave and clad in iron might?
What is a hero?
Fearless, hungry for the fight?
What is a hero?
Hunting legend's beasts?
What is a hero?
Honoured at the feast?
No, this is not a hero,
Nor evermore will be.
A hero's worth lays deep inside.
In places we can't see.
This is a hero
A heart that's honest, good and true
This is a hero
Who'll do his very best for you
This is a hero
By your side till journey's end.
This is a hero,
Simply this. A kind and loyal friend.'

Arthur the Poet

When Arthur finished, everyone was really quiet. Mrs Wendell-Jones had tears in her eyes as she went off to talk to Mr Jenkins about who should win.

After a few minutes, she stepped forward.

'I'm sure you would like to join me in a big round of applause for all of our contestants,' she said. Everyone clapped, then Mrs Wendell-Jones invited all the poets to join her so that she could read out the winner of this year's crown.

'It has been a very difficult contest this year,' she said, 'so many lovely, different poems, but the winner is…'

There was a huge pause. Soppy stepped forwards, a big grin on her face. I could see her opening her mouth, ready to say, *'Oh thank you!'* as she always does.

'Arthur!' called out Mrs Wendell-Jones.

Arthur grinned from ear to ear. Soppy's eyes were as big as saucers. She's never lost anything before. I felt a bit sorry for her then. Maybe being perfect all the time is just as hard as being rubbish at everything. I gave Soppy a 'thumbs up' to let her know that it was OK to lose stuff sometimes.

Mrs Wendell-Jones opened a wooden box on a table at the side of the stage and took out the battered Eisteddfod Crown. Arthur's eyes shone as she walked across the stage towards him and placed it firmly on his head.

'Well, there's a thing,' she said. 'It's normally far too big, but it fits you like a glove.'

There was a huge burst of applause and cheering from the side of the stage. It was the knights, all whooping and waving at Arthur.

Chapter Fifteen

The Joust

'That was amazing!' I told Arthur.

Arthur grinned and put his hand up to touch the crown on his head.

'I couldn't have done it without you, Tomos,' he said. 'Thank you for helping me win my crown back.'

'But I didn't do anything,' I said. 'I just kept nagging you to help me to joust.'

Arthur shook his head.

'You stood up to Lancelot and Galahad,' he said. 'You were brave and honourable and tried to help me, even though there were twelve of them and only one of you. You showed me what a real hero is.

That's what I put into my poem, and that's why I won.'

I thought Arthur was being a bit too nice.

'I don't feel like much of a hero,' I said.

Arthur looked at me very sternly. 'Tomos,' he ordered, 'kneel down.'

I did as he said, feeling a bit daft. Then, from the folds of his great cloak, Arthur drew Excalibur, the legendary sword that Mrs Wendell-Jones had told us all about. The one that had been taken out of a melon to make Arthur king. Arthur lifted it into the air and then brought it down, first on one of my shoulders and then the other.

'I dub thee, Sir Tomos of Harlech,' Arthur said.

OH WOW!!!!

All the knights applauded and Lancelot helped me get back on my feet.

'You are a great hero,' Arthur said to me, 'and whether you win that joust or not, you will always be the worthiest knight I've ever known.'

Gwion Gruffudd was already at the jousting lane when I arrived, doing lots of elaborate stretches. His armour was super-shiny. He said it was bought in Cardiff and had been made specially to fit him. I didn't care. Mum had done a really good job with mine, even though some of the paint was beginning to flake off my boots. I picked up my noodle-lance and wheeled my bicycle over to the end of the lane.

'Ready to be beaten, huh, Jones?' Gwion shouted at me.

I pulled myself up as tall as I could manage (which isn't much) and climbed onto my bike, ready for the joust to begin. Mr Deacon picked up a trumpet with a flag hanging off the end and shouted, 'When I sound the trumpet, competitors may begin.'

Gwion glared at me and leaned forwards on his bike.

I drew a deep breath and said, 'Don't look at him, don't look at him,' over and over.

Mr Deacon lifted the trumpet to his lips ... and we were off.

Gwion raced down the lane towards me, shrieking as loud as he could. I was so startled that I looked straight at him and started to wobble on my bike. As Gwion soared past me he easily knocked me off my bike.

'First pass to Gwion Gruffudd,' Mr Deacon called out. Mair Gruffudd cheered and laughed and shouted something rude that made Mrs Wendell-Jones tell her off.

I limped back to the starting line. I'd twisted my knee and my armour was hanging off my shoulder at an odd angle.

The second time I was ready for Gwion's shrieking. I managed to avoid looking at him and threw my lance-noodle out at just the right time to catch him on the edge of his helmet. The ball velcroed to the top wobbled a bit and then fell off. Mair booed and Mrs Wendell-Jones gave her detention.

'Second pass to Tomos Jones,' Mr Deacon called out. 'The next challenge is the decider.'

'You might as well give up now, Jones!' Gwion yelled. 'That last one was lucky. But don't worry – I'll be thinking of you when I'm watching *PowerUp!*'

I started to get that feeling again, like I wanted to run away and hide. I was about to get beaten by Gwion Gruffudd in front of the entire school and there was no way he would ever let me forget it.

'Look at him!' Gwion jeered, 'He's afraid. Scaredy cat. Chicken. Squawk!!!!!' and he started to make chicken noises and strut about up and down the jousting lane. A few of the kids laughed and some joined in.

Scaredy cat.

Chicken.

I started to remember something. Something about…

…the *CHICKEN!!!!*

Of course! Merlin's killer chicken! It hadn't really been dangerous, but Merlin had made everyone scared of it by pretending it was. And it hadn't really been  outside my shed, but I managed to scare the knights by pretending it was. Well, now I was going to pretend more than I had ever pretended in my life. If I could pretend I was a great knight, maybe I could make Gwion believe it. Maybe I could even make *myself* believe it.

I was going to give Gwion Gruffudd something to be scared of.

If I was a chicken, I was going to be **The Chicken of Doom!**

I brandished my noodle-lance in the air and shouted as loudly as I could.

'Yes, it is I,' I yelled. 'Sir Tomos of Harlech. The great and mighty vanquisher of the Round Table and personal friend of Arthur, King of the Britons.'

Mrs Wendell-Jones clapped her hands with delight. 'Oh, how wonderful, Tomos,' she cried. 'Really getting into the spirit of things.'

Gwion looked puzzled. He didn't quite know what I was up to.

'I will challenge you, puny squire, and I will win,' I shouted. All the knights started cheering and crying, 'All hail Sir Tomos,' and, 'Go get him!'

Gwion glared at me. We both clambered onto our bicycles and faced each other down the long jousting lane. Mr Deacon seemed to take an age to blow the trumpet and then I was speeding towards Gwion. The knights were shouting loudly for me and stamping their feet on the ground so much that it thundered and drowned out Gwion's battle cries. I kept my face firmly facing front, just glimpsing Gwion coming towards me on my left side. I waited till he was almost within reach and then I swung my noodle-lance as hard as I possibly could, throwing all my weight behind it.

I felt the lance swish through the air, the jolt as it hit Gwion, and then the lance rebounded round as I carried on down the lane. The crowd was cheering.

They were cheering my name!

I stopped my bike, gasping for breath, and looked behind me. In the middle of the jousting lane, Gwion Gruffudd was sitting on the floor looking furious.

I had won.

Chapter Sixteen

Crowns are unnecessary

It was just sinking in when the knights surrounded me and hoisted me up in the air chanting, 'Tom-os, Tom-os!!!' Everyone was clapping and cheering. Sharon Jones gave me the big thumbs up and Alan Pritchard put his little fingers in his mouth and let off a piercing whistle. Even Soppy looked a bit proud of me, punched me on the shoulder and said, 'Well done, squirt.'

Mrs Wendell-Jones picked her way through the crowd and smiled at Lancelot.

'He did splendidly, didn't he,' she said. 'Now if you could just put him down we'll sort out the prize-giving.'

The prize-giving! In all the excitement I'd almost forgotten what all this was for – the chance to meet *PowerUp*. Mrs Wendell-Jones led me up onto the podium and waved her hands to get everyone to quieten down.

'I'm sure you'll all agree that we've had a fantastic day,' she said. 'Young Tomos is our jousting champion and his prize is to meet *PowerUp* when he goes to their next concert.' She handed me an envelope and said. 'There you are, Tomos, you've earned this. You must have worked very hard.'

'I had a bit of help, miss,' I admitted, grinning at Arthur.

I felt brilliant. I turned to find Mum and Dad and they were looking at me like they looked at Soppy, like I'd done something really special for once.

As Mrs Wendell-Jones and I walked off the stage, she said, 'One more thing, Tomos, may I have a word about your essay?'

Uh-oh, just when I was feeling really good about myself.

'I've been having a word with Mr Lance,' she said, pointing at Lancelot, who tossed his hair and winked at Mrs Wendell-Jones.

'Well,' she continued, 'Mr Lance, it appears, is something of an expert in Arthurian works, and he informs me that there are some recently discovered texts which support the more … ah … unusual parts of your essay, so I will have to bow to expert opinion and regrade your essay, Tomos.'

She handed me a piece of paper. It was my report card. I turned it over to see what I got for my end of term essay. I looked down the list of marks and saw all those dreadful Cs (and worse) and there, at the bottom was an

A!!!!

Oh wow! My first ever A!

I was about to thank Mrs Wendell-Jones, but Arthur came over and tapped me on the shoulder.

'Urm, Tomos, we are thinking that it is about time we went,' he said.

'Oh that is a shame,' Mrs Wendell-Jones said. 'Well, you'd better give me the Eisteddfod crown back then.'

Arthur frowned.

'My crown?' he said.

Oh no. He thought he'd get to keep it.

'You can't take it with you,' I explained. 'It has to go back in the trophy cupboard.'

'So what do I get?' Arthur asked.

'A certificate.'

Arthur was horrified.

'But it's my crown. Without my crown, I'm … well, I'm…'

'Our King!' came a cry from behind us. 'Tomos was right. A king without a crown is still a King.'

Then all the knights knelt down and bowed their heads to Arthur.

King Arthur.

Their King.

Arthur beamed from ear to ear. Then he took his crown off, gave it one last polish with his sleeve and handed it over to Mrs Wendell-Jones.

'It was nice having it back for a little while,' he said, but Mrs Wendell-Jones didn't understand.

'Do you have to go so soon?' I asked Arthur as we all walked towards the gate of the castle. He nodded.

'My kingdom no longer needs me,' he said, smiling down at me. 'You won it all, Tomos. The joust, the respect of your classmates. You won it because you believe in yourself, and that's good. There is a lot to believe in.'

'You're just being nice,' I mumbled.

Arthur shook his head. 'You are Sir Tomos of Harlech,' he said. 'Never let anyone tell you otherwise. You are a hero among men.'

The knights gathered round and bowed their heads to me. It hadn't been easy having them all in the shed, but I was really going to miss them.

'We'll be back if you should ever need us, Tomos,' said Lancelot. 'You know, if you need your teacher buttering up.'

'Or you need something fixing,' said Bedevere.

'Or you need the advanced jousting course,' said Gawain.

'What, the one with a horse?' Lancelot joked and they all laughed. Usually when the knights laughed, Arthur looked sad because they were laughing at him, but this time he joined in.

I had a sudden idea.

'I want to give you something,' I said, 'stay there!'

I dashed off and got my bicycle and pushed it over to Arthur.

'Mum and Dad have promised me a new one for my birthday,' I said, 'so I won't be needing this anymore and I thought ... that if you ever get to joust again ... you can use this. Instead of a horse.'

Arthur grinned. 'That's perfect, Tomos,' he cried. 'A mount fit for a king!'

'Tomos,' Lancelot said, 'if you do ever need us, you know where to find us.'

I nodded. 'The secret's safe with me,' I promised.

I looked at Arthur.

'Goodbye, Arthur,' I said. 'Goodbye, King.'

Arthur suddenly gave me a huge hug.

'Goodbye, Tomos,' he said. 'Goodbye, friend.'

Then he and the knights left the castle and began their long trek to their resting place. I stood by the castle gates waving at them till all I could see was their shadows on the horizon. Twelve knights and one king, wobbling towards the hills on my bicycle.